# THE CHRONICLES OF

# NARNIA

## PRINCE CASPIAN

## The Movie Storybook

The Chronicles of Narnia®, Narnia® and all book titles, characters and locales original to
The Chronicles of Narnia are trademarks of C.S. Lewis Pte. Ltd. Use without permission is strictly prohibited.

Prince Caspian: The Movie Storybook
Copyright © 2008 by C.S. Lewis Pte. Ltd.
Art/illustration © 2008 Disney Enterprises, Inc. and Walden Media, LLC.
This edition published in 2008 by HarperCollins Children's Books.
HarperCollins Children's Books is a division of HarperCollins Publishers,
77-85 Fulham Palace Road, Hammersmith, London W6 8JB

www.harpercollinschildrensbooks.co.uk

www.narnia.com

A CIP record for this title is available from the British Library.
ISBN 978-0-00-725835-2

1 3 5 7 9 10 8 6 4 2

Book design by Rick Farley, Sean Boggs and John Sazaklis

Printed in Italy

# THE CHRONICLES OF
# NARNIA
# PRINCE CASPIAN
## The Movie Storybook

Adapted by Lana Jacobs

Based on the screenplay by Andrew Adamson
& Christopher Markus & Stephen McFeely

Based on the book by C. S. Lewis

Directed by Andrew Adamson

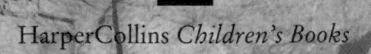

HarperCollins *Children's Books*

Professor Cornelius tiptoed into Prince Caspian's room in the middle of the night. He had to help his student escape the Telmarine soldiers who waited outside his door. Cornelius led Caspian out of the room through the secret passage in the wardrobe.

Just before Cornelius sent Caspian away from the castle on his horse, he handed Caspian a special gift. "Do not use it except at your greatest need. Everything you know is about to change," he said.

Upon discovering Caspian's room empty, the Telmarine soldiers searched the castle. Then they saw Caspian head toward the wood, so the soldiers followed him.

Suddenly, Caspian fell off his horse. He opened his eyes to find three creatures standing above him, two Dwarfs and a Badger. As they closed in on Caspian, he reached into the bag that contained Cornelius's gift . . . and pulled out an ivory horn. Caspian blew into the horn before the Dwarfs had a chance to stop him.

Nikabrik, one of the Dwarfs, knocked Caspian out with his sword. Nikabrik and his friends brought Caspian inside their den to find out more about that small white horn that Caspian carried with him.

Meanwhile, on a train platform in London, the Pevensie children struggled to adjust to ordinary lives filled with schoolbooks and uniforms. They fought with other children at school. They longed to return to their lives as Kings and Queens of Narnia.

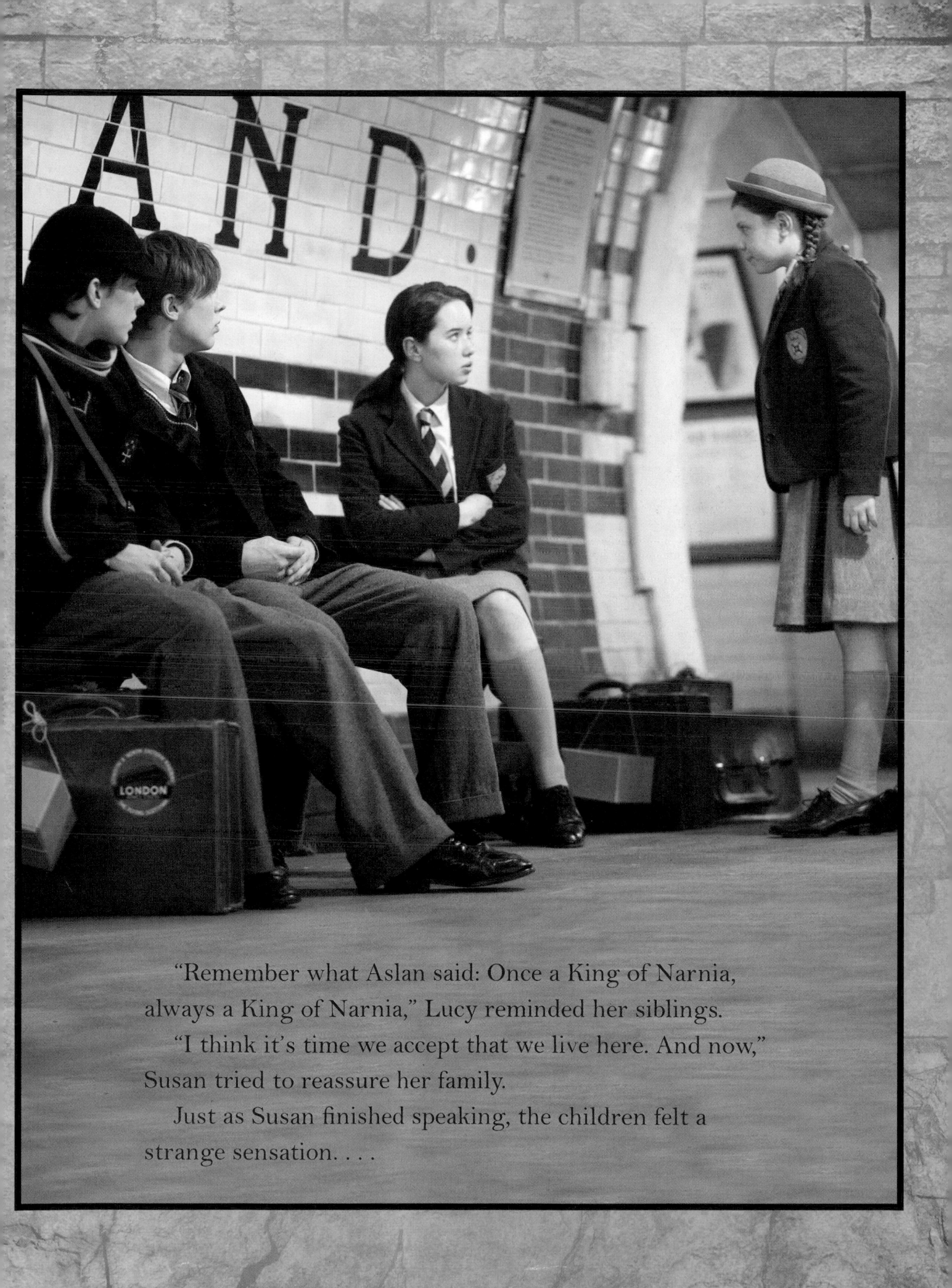

"Remember what Aslan said: Once a King of Narnia, always a King of Narnia," Lucy reminded her siblings.

"I think it's time we accept that we live here. And now," Susan tried to reassure her family.

Just as Susan finished speaking, the children felt a strange sensation. . . .

Moments later, the Pevensies found themselves standing on a white, sandy beach. Their dreams had come true . . . they were back in Narnia! But something in the distance looked unfamiliar. "I don't remember any ruins in Narnia," Edmund said.

Walking toward the ruins, Susan found a golden chess piece on the ground. Suddenly it dawned on Peter: They were standing before Cair Paravel, their former Narnian home.

Back at the castle, King Miraz and his advisors discussed the Prince's disappearance. By blaming everything on the Narnians, Miraz would be justified in starting a war that would allow him to claim the throne as his own. His plan came to life as his soldiers brought in a captured Narnian, a Dwarf.

"We forget that Narnia was once a savage land," Miraz reminded his council. "They've been watching us, waiting to strike—and I intend to strike back," he said as he pointed to the Dwarf.

Unaware of the trouble brewing, the children marvelled at the rubble that was once their glorious Cair Paravel. "This didn't just happen. Cair Paravel was attacked," Edmund declared.

They stumbled upon the treasure chamber, where Lucy found her cordial, Edmund his helmet, Peter his sword and shield and Susan her quiver and bow. The only thing missing was Susan's horn.

"I think it's time we found out what's going on," Peter declared.

Caspian awoke inside Trufflehunter the Badger's den. Caspian
was shocked to hear Trufflehunter and Nikabrik speak . . . they were
living Narnians, creatures from the fairy tales he had heard as a child!

As Caspian turned to leave, Nikabrik stopped him.

"You're meant to save us," Trufflehunter said, the ivory horn sitting nearby. "It is said that whoever sounds it will bring back the Ancient Kings and Queens . . . and lead us to freedom," the Badger explained.

Little did Caspian know that his magical horn had already brought back the Ancient Kings and Queens. Now dressed in Narnian garb, the children set out to learn exactly what had been going on while they were away. They were surprised to find Telmarine soldiers holding a Narnian captive. Susan immediately shot two arrows at the soldiers to save the Dwarf.

"Beards and bedsteads," Trumpkin exclaimed. These children were actually the Kings and Queens of old that he and the rest of the Narnians had been waiting for!

When Caspian met the rest of the Narnians on the Dancing Lawn, the crowd was angry, for they had learned to fear all Telmarines. By showing the horn, Caspian tried to convince them that he could bring peace to Narnia—if they would help him claim his throne from the evil Miraz.

The Narnians didn't
believe Caspian's promise, but
Trufflehunter quickly came
to his aid: "We Badgers
remember well that Narnia
was never right except
when a Son of Adam was
King." The Narnians agreed:
It was time for Caspian to
take his place as King
and restore order to
the land of Narnia.

The Narnians weren't the only ones who longed for the Narnia of old. Lucy was saddened to learn that the trees no longer danced and the Bears were no longer her friends.

As the children crossed the river to enter the wood, Lucy saw something spectacular. "Aslan!" she cried. But nobody saw the Great Lion except for Lucy.

Later that night, Lucy dreamed that she saw Aslan. Upon waking, she headed into the wood. Mistaking a rustling sound for Aslan, Lucy was disappointed to find Peter standing with his sword drawn. Before Lucy could ask Peter what he was doing, Caspian appeared and attacked Peter!

But with Narnians at his side, Lucy knew that the attacker could not be their enemy. Lucy called for the fighting to stop. Peter regarded his opponent.

"Prince Caspian?" Peter asked. "I believe you called?"

"Who are you?" Caspian asked. With that, Susan and Edmund came running into the forest.

The Narnians were happy to see their Kings and Queens of old standing before them.

Prince Caspian brought everyone back to his underground camp, where he and the Narnians had been preparing for battle. "It may not be what you're used to, but it's defensible," he said.

"What is this place?" Lucy asked as she stared at the drawings of herself and her siblings on the wall.

Caspian lit the torch to illuminate Aslan's Stone Table . . . they were standing inside Aslan's How!

The time had come to put Caspian on the throne, and the Narnians were ready. King Peter and the Narnian war council discussed how to attack Miraz's castle.

The Narnian army approached the castle in the middle of the night. "For Narnia!" Peter called as he raised his sword and charged toward the Telmarines.

Peter fought alongside the bravest Narnians: the Satyrs and Fauns. Together they charged ahead.

They battled the Telmarines as best they could, but in the end, the Telmarines forced them to retreat back to Aslan's How.

Peter knew it would take more than spirit to defeat these soldiers—they needed help. They needed Aslan. Peter sent Lucy deep into the forest to find him. The Great Lion quickly appeared before her.

Lucy threw her arms around Aslan, and then asked him why he hadn't come sooner to save them. "Things never happen the same way twice, dear one," he said. "I think your friends have slept long enough, don't you?"

And with that, Aslan woke up the sleeping trees, and headed toward the battle.

Back at the How, Caspian suggested challenging Miraz to a one-on-one duel with Peter. "The fight shall be to the death. The reward shall be total surrender," Edmund proclaimed as he read the decree to Miraz.

Miraz accepted Peter's challenge to a duel. Just as Peter had Miraz cornered, he handed his sword to Caspian, saying that it was not his fight to end.

"Keep your life, but I'm giving the Narnians
back their kingdom," Caspian said as he towered
over Miraz.

Even after Caspian defeated Miraz, the Telmarines
continued to advance upon the Narnians with their
swords drawn high.

"Narnians, charge!" bellowed Peter.

They braced themselves for the attack, but they were no
match for the Telmarines. They needed something more. . . .
Just then, the trees launched their attack on the soldiers!
Peter knew instantly that Lucy had found Aslan.

"For Aslan!" Peter called
as he charged toward the soldiers.

The Telmarines retreated toward the bridge that would lead them out of the wood and away from the Narnians. As the soldiers rushed ahead, Aslan appeared before them. He let out a mighty roar and defeated the soldiers once and for all.

Gathered before a crowd of Narnians, Peter and his siblings dropped to their knees, heads bowed before the mighty Lion.

"Rise, Kings and Queens of Narnia," Aslan said.

He declared Caspian the new King of Narnia, as Peter handed his sword to Caspian.

"I'll hold it until your return," Caspian responded, in awe of this great honour.

The Pevensies took one last look at their beloved, magical land, and then walked through the doorway that Aslan created in a nearby oak tree. On the other side of the doorway, the children found themselves back on the train platform in their school uniforms.